The Snowy Surprise

Based on *The Railway Series* by the Rev. W. Awdry

Illustrations by *Robin Davies*

EGMONT

TO THE TRAINS ➔

This is a story about a very snowy winter's day, when Thomas, Percy and their friends worked together to bring a happy Christmas to a mountain village that was in trouble . . .

Thomas enjoyed puffing up and down his branch line every day. He liked the sights and the people he met along the way.

One of his favourite places to visit was a small village, high in the mountains. The people there were very friendly, and always waved to Thomas as he passed.

On Christmas Eve, the engines woke to find that a winter storm was covering Sodor with a thick blanket of snow.

The Fat Controller came to see Thomas and Percy. "Percy, you will take Thomas' coaches and deliver the Christmas post along his branch line today," he said. "I need Thomas at the Docks."

Thomas was disappointed. He wanted to see if his friends in the village needed help in the storm.

"I'll look after your friends for you!" Percy promised.

Percy took Annie and Clarabel and steamed up the mountain. Even in the snow, he was making good time.

Suddenly, his Driver called out, "What's that?"

Through the blizzard, Percy saw a red glow. As he got closer, he saw that it was a Fogman standing by the track with a warning light.

"Every road and track to the village is blocked by the snow," the Fogman shouted. "You must fetch help, Percy!"

"Bouncing buffers!" Percy thought, worriedly. He had promised Thomas he would look after the villagers, and now they were in trouble!

Percy knew just what to do. He left his carriages in a siding and puffed quickly to the Airfield where Harold the Helicopter was resting.

"Peep! Peep!" whistled Percy, loudly. "The roads to the mountain village are blocked with snow. The villagers need our help!"

"Right away!" Harold replied, as he buzzed up into the air and flew off to tell The Fat Controller.

Percy headed back towards the Yard, and he was almost there when he met another engine coming the other way. It was Thomas, wearing a snowplough.

After hearing Percy's message, The Fat Controller had sent Thomas to take Terence the Tractor and a works train to help the people in the village.

"Thank you for looking after my friends, Percy," puffed Thomas. "Now, follow me!"

Percy buffered up behind Thomas' heavy train, helping to push it up the mountain. Thomas' snowplough cleared the snow from the tracks that led to the village.

Thomas and Percy had to go very slowly. When they tried to go faster, their wheels slipped and spun on the icy rails.

Working together, Thomas and Percy struggled up the steep mountain.

At last, Thomas puffed, "There's the village!"

Percy was very tired, but he pushed and pushed until the train was safely in the station.

Percy heard a loud buzzing from the air, and looked up. He was happy to see Harold dropping parcels of food for the people and their pets in the village.

Terence the Tractor quickly got to work. With his strong caterpillar tracks and snowplough, he cleared the snow so that people could walk safely and drive their cars.

"Snow is lovely stuff!" said Terence, cheerfully, as he worked.

The children agreed. They were having fun sledging down the hills and making snowmen in the village.

At last, the snowstorm passed. Terence ploughed the last road in the village and then rolled back onto Thomas' flatbed.

Percy went to fetch Annie and Clarabel from the siding so that the villagers would have their letters and presents in time for Christmas.

By the time he returned, Toby had arrived with Henrietta. They had brought hot chocolate and mince pies for the tired workmen and villagers.

As Thomas and Percy chuffed away, the villagers waved goodbye. "Well done, Percy! Well done, Thomas!" they cried. "Thank you for giving us a happy Christmas!"

Thomas and Percy smiled. They had never felt more like Really Useful Engines.

When Thomas and Percy were out of sight, the villagers talked about a way to thank the engines for their hard work. They made a wonderful plan.

That night, the villagers loaded many boxes and parcels into Henrietta, then climbed aboard. Toby puffed through the snowy countryside and steamed into the Yard as quietly as he could. Thomas and Percy were fast asleep after their very busy day.

The villagers took their boxes and parcels, and tiptoed into the shed. Toby didn't know what the villagers were going to do, but it was sure to be a splendid surprise!

Thomas was the first to wake up on Christmas morning. He could not believe his eyes!

"Peep, peep!" he whistled in surprise.

The others woke, too, and all looked round in wonder. The shed had been magically decorated with tinsel and fairy lights. There was even a Christmas tree with lots of presents underneath!

Thomas and his friends whistled in delight.

"It is a Really Merry Christmas for everyone!" said Percy, and they all agreed!

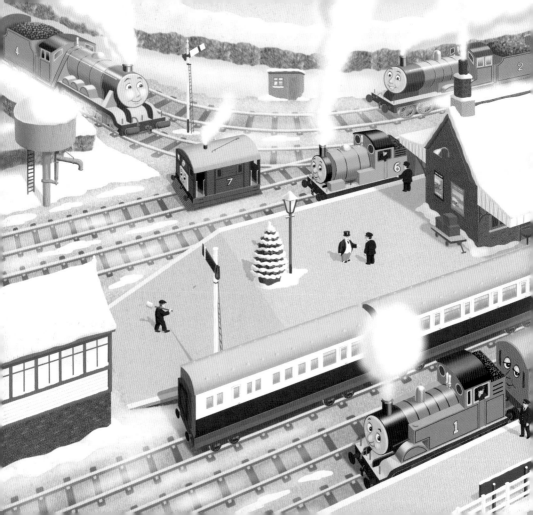

Thomas Story Library

 Thomas
 Edward
 Henry
 Gordon
 James
 Percy
 Toby

 Emily
 Alfie
 Annie and Clarabel
 'Arry and Bert
 Arthur
 Bertie
 Bill and Ben

Peep!
Peep!

 BoCo
 Bulgy
 Charlie
 Cranky

 Daisy
 Dennis
 Diesel
 Donald and Douglas

 Duck

 Duncan

 The Fat Controller

 Fergus

 Freddie

 George

 Harold

 Hector

 Hiro

 Jack

 Jeremy

 Kevin

 Mighty Mac

 Murdoch

 Oliver

 Peter Sam

 Rocky

 Rosie

 Rusty

 Salty

 Sir Handel

 Skarloey

 Spencer

 Stepney

 Terence

 Trevor

 Troublesome Trucks

 Victor